E
H

Harness, Cheryl.

Ghosts of the Civil
War.

/Older Reader   AN 7   2002

DATE			

12/04   1/13
            5X
+ 2   9 L
L=18   4/08

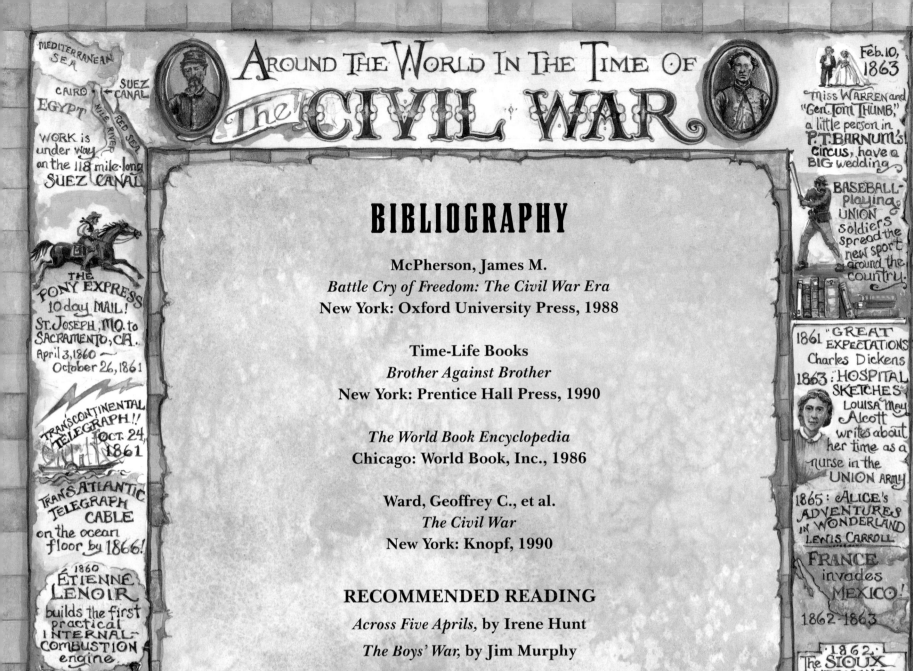

AROUND THE WORLD IN THE TIME OF The CIVIL WAR

Left margin

MEDITERRANEAN SEA

CAIRO · SUEZ CANAL

EGYPT · NILE RIVER · RED SEA

WORK is under way on the 118 mile long SUEZ CANAL

THE PONY EXPRESS 10 day MAIL! ST. JOSEPH, MO. to SACRAMENTO, CA. April 3, 1860 — October 26, 1861

TRANSCONTINENTAL TELEGRAPH!! OCT. 24, 1861

TRANSATLANTIC TELEGRAPH CABLE on the ocean floor by 1866!

1860 ÉTIENNE LENOIR builds the first practical INTERNAL COMBUSTION engine.

People are hard at work on the TRANSCONTINENTAL RAILROAD.

Right margin

Feb. 10, 1863 "Miss WARREN and "Gen. TOM THUMB," a little person in P. T. BARNUM'S CIRCUS, have a BIG wedding

BASEBALL-playing UNION soldiers spread the new sport around the country.

1861 "GREAT EXPECTATIONS" Charles Dickens

1863: HOSPITAL SKETCHES LOUISA MAY Alcott writes about her time as a nurse in the UNION ARMY

1865: ALICE'S ADVENTURES IN WONDERLAND LEWIS CARROLL

FRANCE invades MEXICO! 1862-1863

1862. The SIOUX UPRISING Starving LAKOTA people raid and kill white settlers in MINNESOTA. President LINCOLN orders the hangings of 38 INDIAN leaders.

Bottom margin

Queen Victoria reigns over the Empire of GREAT BRITAIN 1837-1901

1860-1861 Guisseppe GARIBALDI leads 1,000 "RED SHIRTS" in battle to unite his country: THE KINGDOM of ITALY is formed.

1861 CZAR ALEXANDER II frees the SERFS, Russian peasants bound to work land owned by the aristocrats.

EMPRESS Tzu-Hsi reigns (1862-1908) over a troubled CHINA millions die in bloody uprisings. 1851-1864

Center

BIBLIOGRAPHY

McPherson, James M.
Battle Cry of Freedom: The Civil War Era
New York: Oxford University Press, 1988

Time-Life Books
Brother Against Brother
New York: Prentice Hall Press, 1990

The World Book Encyclopedia
Chicago: World Book, Inc., 1986

Ward, Geoffrey C., et al.
The Civil War
New York: Knopf, 1990

RECOMMENDED READING

Across Five Aprils, by Irene Hunt

The Boys' War, by Jim Murphy

Soldier's Heart, by Gary Paulsen

The Red Cap and *Mr. Lincoln's Drummer,* by G. Clifton Wisler

GLOSSARY

Abolitionist: Someone who thought slavery should be abolished (done away with).

The Cause: Folks' reasons for fighting. For Northerners it was, generally, the Union, one nation, undivided. Telling the people that they were fighting to free the slaves was not something Lincoln the politician could easily do—not until after the Emancipation Proclamation in January 1863, anyway. Liberty and justice for all has always been the hardest part. In the South "the Glorious Cause" was the idea that under the umbrella of a central government, states (the people) ought to be able govern themselves—and get out from under the umbrella if they chose to. Of course, there were about four million black Southerners for whom self-government was only a dream.

Confederate: Someone fighting for, or a member of, the Confederate States of America (CSA), the government formed by the eleven Southern states that left the Union in 1860 and 1861. Two other border states, Kentucky and Missouri, also had Confederate governments.

Contraband: What former slaves who had come over to the Union army were called. Before the war it was federal law to return runaway slaves to their master.

Dixie: The land south of the Mason-Dixon Line (the border was between Maryland and Pennsylvania, and was used to separate the slave and free states before the war). The song "Dixie" was written in 1859 by Ohio-born Daniel D. Emmett.

Free-Soil: The idea that slavery should not extend into new U.S. territories or states, such as Kansas or Nebraska. The Free-Soil Party started in 1848. It was part of the big North-South split that led to the beginning of the Republican Party in the 1850s.

Rangers: Far from the battlefields bold rangers on horseback raided supply stores, burned barns, wrecked railroads and bridges, and made life rotten for civilians. The best-known Confederate rangers were Colonel John Singleton Mosby, known as "the Gray Ghost," and General John Hunt Morgan. Union General Philip Sheridan turned the Shenandoah Valley into a wasteland. Thanks to such bushwhackers as William Quantrill and "Bloody Bill" Anderson, and jayhawkers like Jim Lane and Doc Jennison, this sort of thing had gone on in Kansas and Missouri since 1855.

Rebel: Someone who breaks away from the established government. Southern fighters were called Rebs, Johnny Rebs, or Seceshers.

Reenactment: When people get together to act out a historic battle or event. It's a way for people to try to experience and understand the past.

Reconstruction: President Lincoln wanted to let the beaten South "up easy." However, after his death the Republican Congress passed strict laws to bring the Southern states back into the Union, get some revenge, and protect the rights of former slaves (for a while, anyway) in spite of the sometimes-violent resistance of white Southerners. Federal troops didn't pull out of the South until 1877.

Secession: Formal withdrawal from an organization. Confederates thought they had the right to withdraw from the Federal Union of States.

Sutler: A storekeeper or merchant who sold food, playing cards, pocket Bibles, and other goods to soldiers.

***Uncle Tom's Cabin*:** An 1852 novel written by Harriet Beecher Stowe (1811-1896). It dramatized the evils of slavery and got people so spun up that when she met President Lincoln, he said, "So you're the little woman who wrote the book that made this great war."

The Underground Railroad: The escape route from the slave states to freedom in the North.

Yankee: A Northerner. Northern soldiers were also called bluecoats, blue-bellies, Billy Yanks, Federals, or Lincolnites.

Zouave: French/Algerian infantrymen. Some volunteer units chose the bright uniforms inspired by the Zouave troops.

The U.S. flag had **33 Stars** in the first 3 months of the Civil War, **34 Stars** 1861-1863 after KANSAS was admitted to the UNION, and **35 Stars** after 1863 when West Virginia was added. NEVADA (Oct. 1864) made 36.

THE UNITED STATES "Stars and Stripes"

1st flag of the CONFEDERACY. The "Stars and Bars"

The "STARS & BARS" had 7 stars for the first 7 states to leave the UNION. This flag looked too much like the U.S. flag — confusing in a battle — so a 2nd one was adopted. But it looked too much like a white flag of surrender — confusing in a battle! — So a red bar was added to the Confederate flag in 1865.

2ND flag of the C.S.A. 1863-1865 13 stars (11 states plus secession governments of KENTUCKY and MISSOURI) Some versions of the 1st flag had 13 stars too.

The battle flag was designed by Gen. Pierre Gustave T. BEAUREGARD after the FIRST BATTLE of MANASSAS (BULL RUN) in 1861. Because of the lives and times it represents, the battle flag inspires strong feelings to this very day.

CONFEDERATE battle flag

3RD national flag of the C.S.A.

How the soldiers were organized

82 PRIVATES	1 CAPTAIN
1 WAGONER	1 1ST LIEUTENANT
2 MUSICIANS	1 2ND LIEUTENANT
8 CORPORALS	1 1ST SERGEANT
+ 4 SERGEANTS	

1 COMPANY

3 to 5 COMPANIES = 1 BATTALION
2 BATTALIONS = 1 REGIMENT commanded by a COLONEL
3 to 5 REGIMENTS = 1 BRIGADE
2 to 5 BRIGADES = 1 DIVISION
2 or 3 DIVISIONS = 1 CORPS (pronounced "core")
1 or more CORPS = an ARMY

Soldiers were organized in other ways too, such as INFANTRY (foot soldiers), CAVALRY (soldiers mounted on horses), and ARTILLERY (men who fired cannons and other guns too big to carry). Sailors fought in the FEDERAL and CONFEDERATE NAVIES.

"I don't believe we can have an army without music."
Gen. Robert E. Lee

Dozens of different bugle calls and drumrolls regulated the soldiers' day. NORTH or SOUTH, they had their spirits lifted by brass bands and drum corps. Musicians also served as medical assistants. But sometimes they made music in battle, "...polkas and waltzes, which sounded very curious, accompanied by the hissing and bursting of the shells," said one observer.

THE arts of death and military tactics were revolutionized in the **CIVIL WAR**, the **FIRST MODERN WAR**

FIRST practical machine gun

FIRST use of railroad trains as a major means of moving troops, supplies, and artillery

FIRST extensive use of trenches (soldiers fighting undercover in deep, narrow ditches)

FIRST extensive use of land mines, "subterranean shells"

FIRST torpedoes

FIRST multi-manned combat submarine

FIRST portable telegraph units on the battlefield

FIRST military reconnaissance (information gathering) from a manned balloon

FIRST draft (people ordered into the military) and FIRST income tax

FIRST photographs taken in combat

FIRST military signaling with flags and torches in battle

walnut stock — hammer — rear sight — steel barrel — blade sight — lock plate — trigger — ram rod

U.S. Model 1861 .58 caliber SPRINGFIELD RIFLE-MUSKET

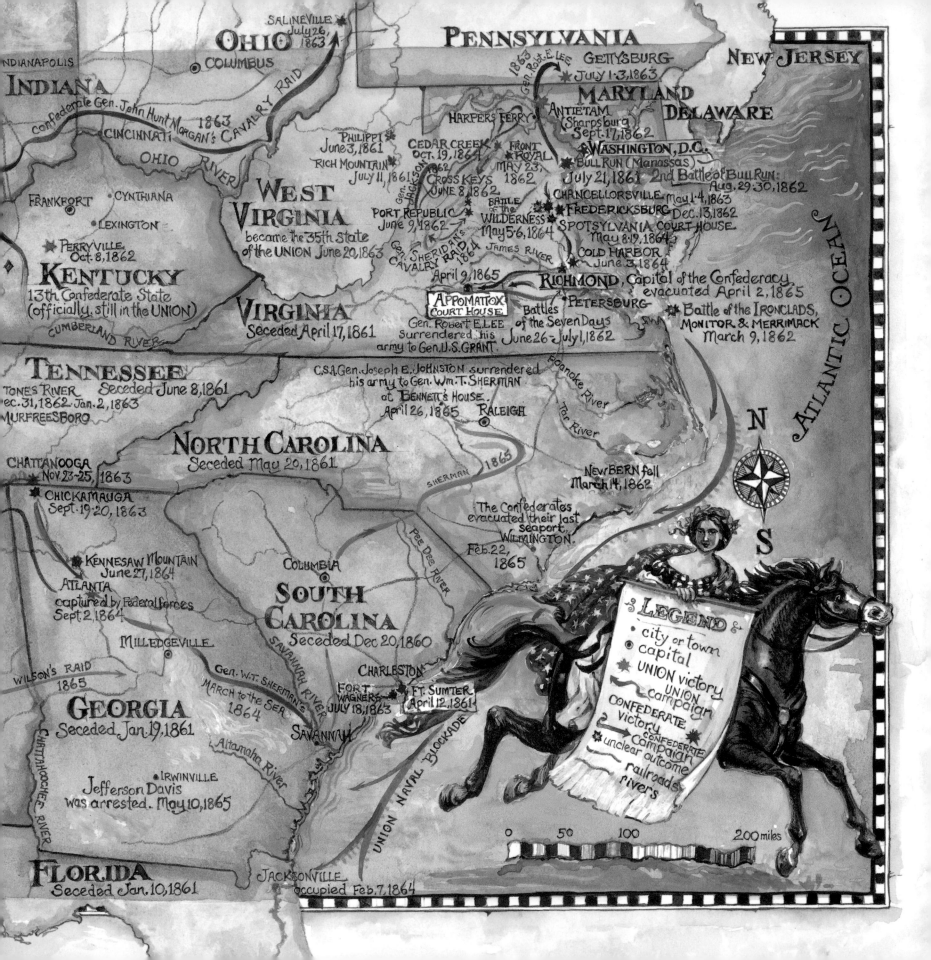

OHIO
SALINEVILLE
July 26, 1863

COLUMBUS

INDIANAPOLIS

INDIANA

Confederate Gen. John Hunt Morgan's Cavalry Raid 1863

CINCINNATI

OHIO RIVER

FRANKFORT • CYNTHIANA
• LEXINGTON

PERRYVILLE
Oct. 8, 1862

KENTUCKY
13th Confederate State
(officially, still in the UNION)

CUMBERLAND RIVER

WEST
VIRGINIA
became the 35th state
of the UNION June 20, 1863

PHILIPPI
June 3, 1861
RICH MOUNTAIN
July 11, 1861

Gen. Jackson 1862
CROSS KEYS
June 8, 1862
PORT REPUBLIC
June 9, 1862→

Gen. SHERIDAN'S
CAVALRY RAID 1864
April 9, 1865

VIRGINIA
Seceded April 17, 1861

APPOMATTOX
COURT HOUSE
Gen. Robert E. Lee
surrendered his
army to Gen. U.S. GRANT.

PENNSYLVANIA

1863 Gen. Robt. E. Lee

GETTYSBURG
July 1-3, 1863

NEW JERSEY

HARPERS FERRY •

CEDAR CREEK
Oct. 19, 1864
FRONT
ROYAL
MAY 23,
1862

ANTIETAM
(Sharpsburg)
Sept. 17, 1862

MARYLAND
DELAWARE

WASHINGTON, D.C.

BULL RUN (Manassas)
July 21, 1861   2nd Battle of Bull Run:
Aug. 29-30, 1862

CHANCELLORSVILLE May 1-4, 1863
FREDERICKSBURG Dec. 13, 1862
SPOTSYLVANIA COURT HOUSE
May 8-19, 1864

BATTLE
OF THE
WILDERNESS
May 5-6, 1864

JAMES RIVER

COLD HARBOR
June 3, 1864

RICHMOND, Capital of the Confederacy,
evacuated April 2, 1865

• PETERSBURG

Battles
of the Seven Days
June 26-July 1, 1862

Battle of the IRONCLADS,
MONITOR & MERRIMACK
March 9, 1862

ATLANTIC OCEAN

TENNESSEE
Seceded June 8, 1861

STONES RIVER
Dec. 31, 1862-Jan. 2, 1863
MURFREESBORO

CHATTANOOGA
Nov. 23-25, 1863

CHICKAMAUGA
Sept. 19-20, 1863

KENNESAW MOUNTAIN
June 27, 1864

ATLANTA
captured by Federal forces
Sept. 2, 1864

MILLEDGEVILLE

WILSON'S RAID
1865

CHATTAHOOCHEE RIVER

GEORGIA
Seceded Jan. 19, 1861

Jefferson Davis
was arrested. May 10, 1865

• IRWINVILLE

Altamaha River

SAVANNAH RIVER

Gen. W.T. SHERMAN'S
MARCH TO THE SEA
1864

SAVANNAH

FLORIDA
Seceded Jan. 10, 1861

JACKSONVILLE
occupied Feb. 7, 1864

C.S.A. Gen. Joseph E. JOHNSTON surrendered
his army to Gen. Wm. T. SHERMAN
at BENNETT'S HOUSE.
April 26, 1865   • RALEIGH

NORTH CAROLINA
Seceded May 20, 1861

SHERMAN 1865

Roanoke River

Tar River

NewBERN fell
March 14, 1862

The Confederates
evacuated their last
seaport,
WILMINGTON.
Feb. 22,
1865

Pee Dee River

COLUMBIA

SOUTH
CAROLINA
Seceded Dec. 20, 1860

CHARLESTON

FORT
WAGNER
July 18, 1863

FT. SUMTER
April 12, 1861

UNION NAVAL BLOCKADE

N
S

LEGEND
• city or town
◉ capital
✹ UNION victory
UNION
campaign
✹ CONFEDERATE
victory
CONFEDERATE
campaign
✦ unclear outcome
railroads
rivers

0   50   100   200 miles

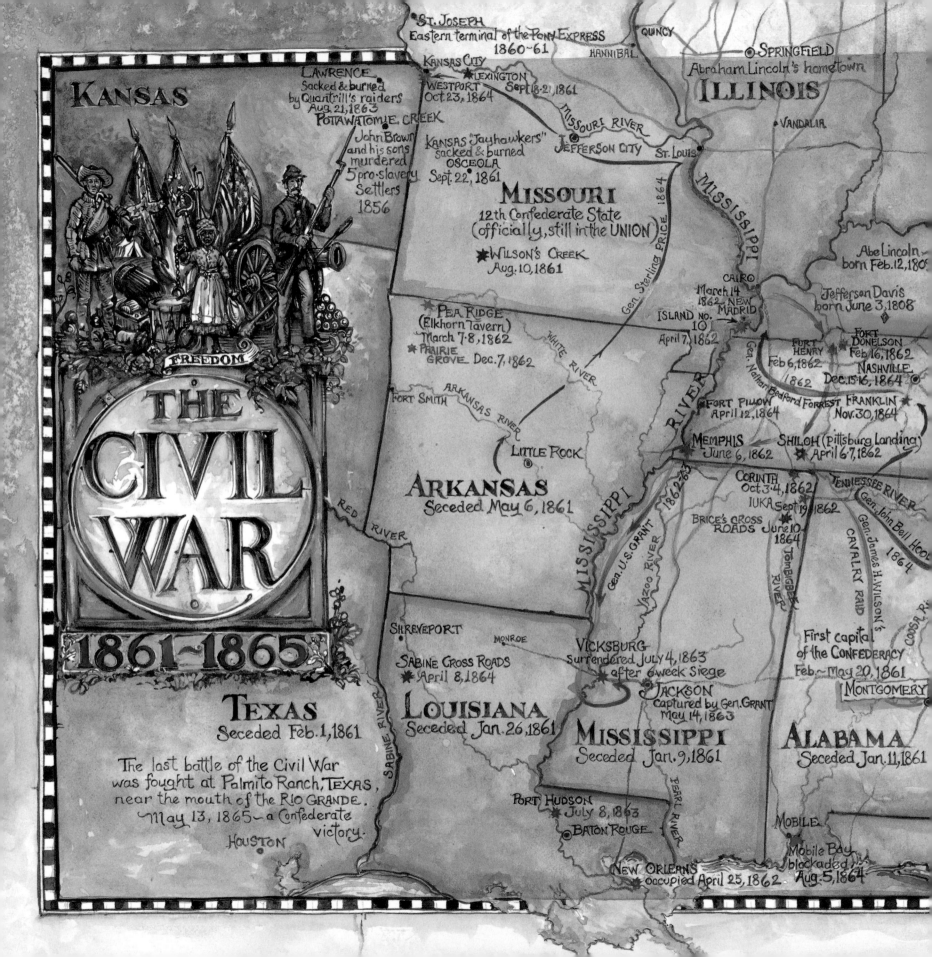

KANSAS

THE CIVIL WAR

1861-1865

FREEDOM

ST. JOSEPH
Eastern terminal of the PONY EXPRESS
1860~61

QUINCY

HANNIBAL

KANSAS CITY

SPRINGFIELD
Abraham Lincoln's hometown

ILLINOIS

LAWRENCE
Sacked & burned
by Quantrill's raiders
Aug. 21, 1863

WESTPORT
Oct. 23, 1864

LEXINGTON
Sept 18-21, 1861

VANDALIA

POTTAWATOMIE CREEK
John Brown
and his sons
murdered
5 pro-slavery
Settlers
1856

Kansas "Jayhawkers"
sacked & burned
OSCEOLA
Sept. 22, 1861

MISSOURI RIVER

JEFFERSON CITY

ST. LOUIS

MISSOURI
12th Confederate State
(officially, still in the UNION)

Wilson's Creek
Aug. 10, 1861

Gen. Sterling Price 1864

MISSISSIPPI

Abe Lincoln
born Feb. 12, 1809

PEA RIDGE
(Elkhorn Tavern)
March 7-8, 1862

PRAIRIE
GROVE Dec. 7, 1862

WHITE RIVER

CAIRO

ISLAND NO.
10
April 7, 1862

March 14
1862 NEW
MADRID

Jefferson Davis
born June 3, 1808

FORT SMITH

ARKANSAS RIVER

LITTLE ROCK

ARKANSAS
Seceded May 6, 1861

RED RIVER

FORT
HENRY
Feb 6, 1862

Gen. Nathan Bedford Forrest

FORT PILLOW
April 12, 1864

MEMPHIS
June 6, 1862

FORT
DONELSON
Feb 16, 1862

NASHVILLE
Dec. 15-16, 1864

FRANKLIN
Nov. 30, 1864

SHILOH (Pittsburg Landing)
April 6-7, 1862

RIVER

1862

CORINTH
Oct. 3-4, 1862

IUKA Sept 19, 1862

BRICE'S CROSS
ROADS June 10
1864

TENNESSEE RIVER

Gen. U.S. GRANT 1862-63

MISSISSIPPI

YAZOO RIVER

Gen. John Bell Hood
1864

TOMBIGBEE RIVER

CAVALRY RAID

Gen. James H. Wilson's

SHREVEPORT

MONROE

VICKSBURG
Surrendered July 4, 1863
after 6 week siege

First capital
of the CONFEDERACY
Feb. ~ May 20, 1861

COOSA R.

SABINE CROSS ROADS
April 8, 1864

JACKSON
captured by Gen. Grant
May 14, 1863

MONTGOMERY

TEXAS
Seceded Feb. 1, 1861

LOUISIANA
Seceded Jan. 26, 1861

MISSISSIPPI
Seceded Jan. 9, 1861

ALABAMA
Seceded Jan. 11, 1861

The last battle of the Civil War
was fought at Palmito Ranch, TEXAS,
near the mouth of the RIO GRANDE.
May 13, 1865 ~ a Confederate
victory.

HOUSTON

PORT HUDSON
July 8, 1863

BATON ROUGE

PEARL RIVER

MOBILE

Mobile Bay
blockaded
Aug. 5, 1864

NEW ORLEANS
occupied April 25, 1862

SABINE RIVER

South

Jefferson Davis (1808-1889)

He graduated from West Point and fought in the Mexican War, as did most of the officers of the Civil War. In 1861 this former Mississippi senator and secretary of war became the first and last president of the Confederacy. After two years of postwar prison he defended his belief in states' rights for the rest of his long life.

Robert Edward Lee (1807-1870)

"Marse Robert" was a distinguished officer in the U.S. Army who didn't believe in slavery or secession—but to fight against his native Virginia was against his code of honor. His mistakes were in daring too much. After the war he was a college president who urged his fellow Southerners to think of themselves as Americans.

Varina Anne "Winnie" Davis (1864-1898)

She was the baby of the Davis family when the Civil War ended. Southern outrage kept this "Daughter of the Confederacy" from marrying the Yankee she loved; early death made her a tragic symbol of the defeated South.

Richard Rowland Kirkland (1843-1863)

He was a South Carolina "Angel of Mercy" who risked enemy fire to bring water to wounded, freezing Union soldiers who were suffering at Fredericksburg. He died later at Chickamauga, just after his 20th birthday.

Mary Boykin Chesnut (1823-1886)

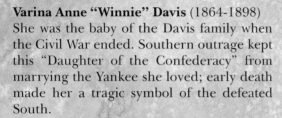

She kept track in a diary of her changing times and the powerful—and powerless—people who passed through her life in South Carolina.

James Ewell Brown Stuart (1833-1864)

Dashing Jeb Stuart was the commander of the cavalry: the "eyes" of General Lee's army. His horsemen could ride like lightning around the enemy troops and find out where they were. He was shot down in a battle with "Little Phil" Sheridan's Union cavalry in 1864.

Nathan Bedford Forrest (1821-1877)

He had 30 horses shot out from under him. He was a fierce genius of cavalry warfare who fought his way from private to general. "War means fightin' and fightin' means killin'," said the so-called Wizard of the Saddle. "If we ain't fightin' to keep slavery, then what the hell are we fightin' for?"

Rose O'Neal Greenhow (1817-1864)

She was not quite as sensational as teenaged Belle Boyd, the "Secesh Cleopatra," but she was a most effective Southern spy in wartime Washington, D.C.

Thomas J. "Stonewall" Jackson (1824-1863)

This iron-willed eccentric general outfoxed the Yankees in the Shenandoah Valley in 1862. He and his hard-marching army of 17,000 Rebels defeated three times as many Federals. More than a century of what-ifs began when he was killed in 1863, just before Gettysburg and the turning point in the Civil War.

Sally Louisa Tompkins (1833-1916)

In her Richmond hospital, in four years of war, 1000 sick and wounded soldiers were cared for. Only 73 of them died: a record! President Davis gave Miss Tompkins the rank of captain in the Confederate cavalry.

NORTH

Abraham Lincoln (1809-1865)

This self-taught lawyer and former Illinois congressman was elected to lead a nation that was tearing itself apart. He used everything he had to save the Union: noble words, a massive army, and wily politics. Days after the Union's victory, "the tiredest man on earth" became the first president to be assassinated.

Ulysses S. Grant (1822-1885)
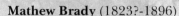
He wasn't the very best president (1869-1877), but shy, decent "Sam" Grant of Ohio was good with horses and war. "I can't spare this man," said Mr. Lincoln, "he fights." Later on, when he was broke and dying, Grant wrote his memoirs (published by Mark Twain) to feed his family—a warrior's last act of courage.

John Brown (1800-1859)
Outlaw radical "Old Osawatomie Brown," an abolitionist, earned his nickname murdering proslavers in Bleeding Kansas, in a righteous cause. He earned fame and the hangman's noose by raiding the federal arsenal at Harpers Ferry in an attempt to raise a slave rebellion.

Mathew Brady (1823?-1896)

He and his assistants took more than 3,500 pictures of the Civil War. They and artists who drew the war, such as Edwin Forbes, Winslow Homer, and the Waud brothers, did what newsreels and TV would do later on: bring the war home.

Anna E. Dickinson (1842-1932)

Thousands, including President Lincoln, came to hear the teenage Quaker "Joan of Arc of the North" give her powerful speeches against slavery and for women's rights.

George B. McClellan (1826-1885)

The Union soldiers owed much to the training they got from this brilliant military man who had everything but a fighting spirit. He's a puzzle who still inspires admiration and fury! He ended up being a railroad executive and the governor of New Jersey.

Frederick Douglass (1818?-1895)

From the time he "stole himself" from slavery in 1838, this author, journalist, passionate orator, and future U.S. minister to Haiti dedicated his life to the full emancipation of people of color.

William Tecumseh Sherman (1820-1891)
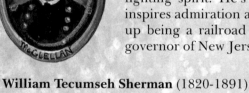
Gloomy "Cump" Sherman of Ohio was one of the few military men who had a pretty good idea just how awful the Civil War was going to be. He helped end it when his Yankee army tore through Georgia and South Carolina like a blue tornado. The man who ended up commanding the entire U.S. Army (after 1869) spoke truly when he said "War is cruelty."

William Lloyd Garrison (1805-1879)

Thirty years before the civil war began, this Boston journalist began publishing *The Liberator*, his influential anti-slavery newspaper. He formed the first society for the immediate end of slavery.

Dr. Mary Edwards Walker (1832-1919)

While Clara Barton was serving as a heroic battlefield nurse, Mary Walker was a pioneer woman doctor. She fought for women's right to vote and dress as they pleased before she was a surgeon with the Union Army, and captured and held as a prisoner of war. After the war she became an author, AND the only woman to receive the medal of honor, the highest military award.

Harriet Tubman (1820?-1913)
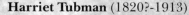
Before she was a heroic Union scout, the woman known as Moses led 300 slaves on 18 dangerous escapes to freedom. She worked for the rest of her difficult life to secure a better future for black Americans.

April 2, 1865
After a last desperate battle, the Army of NORTHERN VIRGINIA gives up PETERSBURG. Gen. Robert E. LEE sends word to President DAVIS that RICHMOND can no longer be saved from Gen. GRANT's armies. Jefferson DAVIS and the rest of the CONFEDERATE government flee the city.

Mobs of people left behind set RICHMOND on fire.

April 3
UNION soldiers, black and white, put out the fires and put the STARS and STRIPES on top of the REBEL capitol. After four long years, the CIVIL WAR is coming to an end.

January 31, 1865

SLAVERY IS ABOLISHED!
(ended) at last

The 13TH Amendment is passed by the U.S. CONGRESS. It becomes the law of the land (ratified) in December 1865 when ¾ of all the states agree.

February 3: President LINCOLN and William H. SEWARD, Secretary of STATE, along with CONFEDERATE Vice President Alexander STEPHENS and other Southern leaders meet on a steamboat at Hampton Roads, VIRGINIA. They talk but fail to agree on a way to end the war.

March 4: Abraham LINCOLN takes his 2ND OATH of OFFICE on INAUGURATION DAY. He tells the people, "...With malice toward none; with charity for all...let us strive on to finish the work we are in; to bind up the nation's wounds ...to do all which may achieve and cherish a just, and a lasting peace among ourselves, and with all nations."

Abe and Mary Lincoln

FEBRUARY 1865: Gen. SHERMAN's ARMY burns and smashes north through SOUTH CAROLINA, punishing the 1st state to secede.

Hurrah!

I s'pected 'im to have horns and a tail, way some white folks talked about 'im!

He looks like the tiredest man on earth, poor soul.

Praise be!

In the end, General Lee and his army couldn't stop General Grant and his. In the end, the Stars and Stripes flew over Richmond, instead of the Rebel Stars and Bars. President Davis had fled the city. It was like the end of a nightmare, four years long. Pa decided to go see Richmond with his own eyes.

Look! Isn't that your little brother?

Yes, Pa liked having Tad close by. Pa sat in Jeff Davis's chair and visited with the wounded soldiers.

Yankee soldiers?

Rebs, too.

The Battle of ANTIETAM

PENNSYLVANIA

GETTYSBURG

HAGERSTOWN

Antietam Creek

Gen. "Stonewall" JACKSON

Potomac River

HARPERS FERRY captured by the SOUTH Sept. 15

Gen. Robert E. LEE takes the WAR into the NORTH

SHENANDOAH RIVER

VIRGINIA

McClellan

LEE

(2nd BULL RUN) MANASSAS JUNCTION Aug. 29-30, a UNION defeat

Gen. George B. McCLELLAN and nearly 80,000 FEDERALS go to meet about 40,000 REBELS in a mighty battle.

WASHINGTON, D.C.

N / W / E / S

USA CSA

0 5 10 15 20 25 miles

SHARPSBURG at, MARYLAND, begins at dawn, September 17, 1862. BY sunset about 23,000 men are wounded, dead, or dying, nearly four times the number of Americans who would be hurt or killed on the NORMANDY beaches on D-DAY 82 years in the future. The day of the Battle at SHARPSBURG remains the bloodiest day in American history.

Gen. LEE and his tattered troops retreated into VIRGINIA. Victorious Gen. McCLELLAN might have chased them and destroyed them, might have ended the terrible CIVIL WAR— but he does not. LEE's army will march into the NORTH one more time.

Up NORTH, the CIVIL WAR is good for business. Manufacturers crank out uniforms, shoes, rifles, and cannons to put down rebellion in the SOUTH AND make money doing it. Food and goods civilians need cost more and more. They are harder to get, especially in the SOUTH where there aren't as many factories; UNION ships keep imports away, and cotton can't be exported. The cost of flour goes as high as $300 per barrel. Newspapers are printed on the back of wallpaper. People follow the progress of the war in publications such as "Frank Leslie's Illustrated Newspaper" and "Harper's Weekly". Folks such as Sarah MORGAN and Mary CHESNUT keep diaries of their own struggles on the homefront. Americans amuse themselves with dances, fairs and baseball, and comfort themselves with songs like "WHEN JOHNNY COMES MARCHING HOME," and "LORENA." They knit socks for soldiers, mourn their dead, and yearn for the day when the cruel war will be over.

PENNSYLVANIA

ANTIETAM CREEK GETTYSBURG

PRO·UNION western counties of VIRGINIA vote to break away from the rest of the state.

SHARPSBURG MARYLAND

After his victory at 2nd MANASSAS, Gen. LEE determines to invade the NORTH!

SECOND BATTLE of BULL RUN (MANASSAS) WASHINGTON D.C.

55,000 Confederates meet 63,000 Federals.

Aug. 29·30, 1862 more than 22,000 men hurt or killed.

Thousands of WOMEN NORTH and SOUTH work as "angels of mercy," caring for the hundreds of thousands of sick and wounded soldiers. The best known to us, is Clara BARTON, who quit her job at the U.S. Patent Office to become a fearless battlefield nurse. In RICHMOND, Sally TOMPKINS runs her small hospital so well that President DAVIS gives her the rank of CAPTAIN. President LINCOLN gives Dr. Mary WALKER, U.S. ARMY surgeon, the MEDAL of HONOR, the only woman to receive this highest military honor.

Legions of ladies like Mary LIVERMORE & Mary Ann "Mother" BICKERDYKE organize food and supplies for the U.S. SANITARY COMMISSION.

Harriet TUBMAN, who had helped nearly 300 people escape from bondage becomes a nurse and scout for the UNION. She bravely gathers information and liberates slaves from behind CONFEDERATE lines.

Not content to stay behind working in their homes, schools, farms, and factories, some women go to WAR as cooks and laundresses OR fellow warriors, like Kady BROWNELL in the NORTH, Amy CLARKE in the SOUTH. They march along and fight beside their husbands. OTHERS, as many as 400, disguise themselves as men and enlist on their own. Jennie HODGERS fights as UNION private "Albert CASHIER."

CONFEDERATE SPIES Belle and Rose GREENHOW, UNION SPY Elizabeth Van LEW, and soldier/spy Sarah Emma EDMONDS are among the many who risked everything in the CIVIL WAR.

DOROTHEA DIX SUPERINTENDENT of female nurses for the UNION

BARTON

TOMPKINS

WALKER

TUBMAN

BICKERDYKE

HODGERS

BOYD

What about gallant girls in the Civil War?

Girls?

Nurse, fetch me that pitcher there, will you, please?

Yes, miss, right away.

Spring and Summer

1862

DAKOTA TERRITORY · MINNESOTA · WISCONSIN · MICHIGAN · NEW YORK · PENNSYLVANIA · CONN.

NEBRASKA TERRITORY · IOWA · OHIO · NEW JERSEY

KANSAS · MISSOURI · ILLINOIS · INDIANA · MARYLAND · DEL.

INDIAN TERRITORY · ARKANSAS · MISSOURI RIVER · OHIO RIVER · KENTUCKY

GEN. "STONEWALL" JACKSON
May 4 – June 9, 1862
SHENANDOAH VALLEY CAMPAIGN

2nd BULL RUN AUG. 29-30

WASHINGTON, D.C.

McCLELLAN'S PENINSULAR CAMPAIGN Mar. 17 – July 3

MCCLELLAN

RICHMOND ★ · STUART · YORKTOWN

VIRGINIA · N. CAROLINA

SEVEN PINES MAY 31 – JUNE 1

BATTLES OF THE SEVEN DAYS June 25 – July 1

LEE

April 6-7, 1862 BATTLE OF SHILOH at PITTSBURG LANDING
U.S. GRANT
TENNESSEE · NASHVILLE
MEMPHIS · CORINTH May 30
JOHNSTON, of the ARMY of the MISSISSIPPI
GEN. DON CARLOS BUELL'S ARMY OF THE OHIO

GEORGIA

S. CAROLINA

Gen. McCLELLAN'S massive UNION army fails to capture RICHMOND because ① he thinks he is hopelessly outnumbered. ② Would-be reinforcements are kept busy fighting JACKSON'S men in the SHENANDOAH. ③ "Jeb" STUART'S cavalry ④ Gen. LEE'S ARMY (+ McCLELLAN'S retreat) save the CONFEDERATE capital in the BATTLES of the 7 DAYS.

CONFEDERATE commander Albert Sidney JOHNSTON is killed at the terrible BATTLE at Pittsburg Landing, Tenn. Gen. P.G.T. BEAUREGARD takes charge of the 45,000 REBELS fighting 65,000 YANKEES led by Generals BUELL and "Unconditional Surrender" GRANT. Nearly 24,000 Americans are hurt or killed in terrible battle: a bloody UNION victory near a little church called SHILOH.

JOHNSTON

MISSISSIPPI RIVER · VICKSBURG · MISSISSIPPI · ALABAMA · PORT HUDSON · MOBILE · NEW ORLEANS April 25, 1862 · LOUISIANA · FLORIDA

FARRAGUT

Flag-Officer David Glasgow FARRAGUT commands a UNION fleet of steam sloops, gunboats, and mortar schooners up into the mouth of the MISSISSIPPI RIVER at the end of April. NEW ORLEANS falls to the UNION and MEMPHIS falls on the 6th of June. VICKSBURG and PORT HUDSON stand fast for the CONFEDERACY – for now.

■ CONFEDERATE STATES of AMERICA
■ UNITED STATES of AMERICA

After Gen. Joe JOHNSTON is wounded at SEVEN PINES, a.k.a. FAIR OAKS, President Jefferson DAVIS chooses Gen. Robert E. LEE to command the ARMY of NORTHERN VIRGINIA.

One of LEE'S generals, J.E.B. STUART, and 1,200 men, gallop 100 miles around the huge UNION army, capturing soldiers, horses, & supplies – making Gen. McCLELLAN nervous. June 12-16, 1862

STUART

WAR IN THE WEST

KANSAS 34TH STATE in the UNION Jan. 29, 1861

WILSON'S CREEK ★ AUG.10,1861

MISSOURI RIVER / MISSISSIPPI RIVER

PEA RIDGE, ARK. MAR. 7-8, 1862

The CONFEDERATES defeat UNION forces at WILSON'S CREEK, MISSOURI. However, the Federals' victory in neighboring ARKANSAS in 1862 keeps MISSOURI – with her important rivers – in the UNION.

In all the states along the border between NORTH & SOUTH, GUERRILLA gangs are unofficial warriors. Young men on horseback lead revenge and pay back raids on civilians, their farms, and towns. Especially in MISSOURI: **TERROR!**

U.S. Senator JAMES LANE leads murderous PRO-UNION "JAYHAWKERS" while guerrilla chieftains William C. QUANTRILL and "Bloody Bill" ANDERSON lead such PRO-SOUTH "BUSHWHACKERS" as Frank and Jesse James.

EXTRA! TRANSCONTINENTAL TELEGRAPH is completed Oct. 24, 1861. The PONY EXPRESS comes to an end after 18 months.

February 1862. Julia Ward Howe's poem is published. "BATTLE HYMN of the REPUBLIC" becomes the great UNION WAR anthem. "Mine eyes have seen the Glory of the coming of the Lord."

ARMY OF THE POTOMAC

CAIRO, ILLINOIS

MISSOURI RIVER / ARKANSAS

Save the UNION strategy: SEIZE CONTROL of the MISSISSIPPI RIVER VALLEY

MISSISSIPPI • MEMPHIS

A grand army is made up of lesser armies. The goal of the ARMY of the POTOMAC, the great UNION army in the EAST, led by Gen. McClellan, is to capture RICHMOND, VIRGINIA, the Confederate capital. The goal of the armies in the WEST is to win control of traffic on AMERICA'S "MAIN STREET," the MISSISSIPPI RIVER.

Who's that? He sure is handsome.

That's General George B. "Little Mac" McClellan. He's mighty smart and proud. Pa chose him to organize and train all the new volunteers into an army to whip the Rebels after they licked us at Bull Run. March and drill, march and drill. I could hear them even when Tad and me were sick in bed.

You were sick?

"TAD" Thomas Lincoln

The USS MERRIMACK, burned and captured by the Confederates, is rebuilt and covered with thick OAK and plates of IRON. The Confederate NAVY call their "ironclad" warship the CSS VIRGINIA.

HURRAH FOR THE CONFEDERACY!
Hurrah for the second American Revolution!
If only they'll let us go in peace and let us run our own lives.
Our own lives.
LIBERTY OR DEATH
DONT TREAD ON ME
MISSISSIPPI January 9, 1861
FLORIDA January 10, 1861
ALABAMA January 11, 1861
GEORGIA January 19, 1861
LOUISIANA January 26, 1861
TEXAS February 1, 1861
VIRGINIA April 17, 1861
ARKANSAS May 6, 1861
NORTH CAROLINA May 20, 1861
TENNESSEE June 8, 1861

The Civil War, the War Between the States, the War of the Rebellion, the Battle of the Blue and the Gray, the Brothers' War, the War for Southern Independence: Whatever it is called, this four years of awfulness touched the life of every American. Ten thousand battles, large and small, plus all manner of sickness, cost more than 600,000 soldiers their lives, and the world all they might have accomplished. They fought with almost unimaginable bravery for their way of life, for the Union, against one another and for one another.

In money and property the war cost more than $15 billion. The whole Southern world of ruined land and cities wouldn't recover until way into the 20th century. After 250 years of slavery 4 million black Americans got their freedom—to fight for a fair deal and their civil rights.

Americans of the 19th century were haunted by the memory of their 18th-century ancestors, who fought a revolution and founded a democratic republic "conceived in liberty," yet which allowed human beings to be held in bondage. There had to be bloody justice. This had to be settled, even if it meant tearing the Union of states apart, so we could be one free nation where we, the people, governed ourselves. But with how much say-so from our leaders in Washington and those closer to home? What does it mean to be a citizen of the United States? And how is one's American life affected by the color of one's skin? It's with these questions that the Ghosts of the Civil War haunt us to this very day.

For Kit and Miss P. T.
I gratefully acknowledge the kind assistance of Mr. Bearrs, Mr. Wisler, and estimable librarians.

It is well that war is so terrible—we should grow too fond of it.

—Robert E. Lee, on watching Union soldiers
charge into gunfire at Fredericksburg, Virginia

SIMON & SCHUSTER BOOKS FOR YOUNG READERS
An imprint of Simon & Schuster Children's Publishing Division
1230 Avenue of the Americas, New York, New York 10020.
Copyright © 2002 by Cheryl Harness.
Book design by Jennifer Reyes. The text for this book is set in 12-point Impress.
The illustrations for this book are rendered in watercolor, ink, and
colored pencil on Strathmore illustration board.
Printed in Hong Kong
2 4 6 8 10 9 7 5 3 1
Library of Congress Cataloging-in-Publication Data
Harness, Cheryl. Ghosts of the Civil War / by Cheryl Harness.
p. cm.
Summary: The ghost of Willie, President Abraham Lincoln's older
son, transports Lindsey back to his own time, where she sees and hears
many things from both sides of the Civil War. Includes passages from
contemporary documents, a glossary, biographical sketches, and a bibliography.
ISBN 0-689-83135-8
1. Lincoln, William Wallace, 1850-1862—Juvenile fiction.
2. United States—History—Civil War, 1861-1865—Juvenile fiction. [1. Lincoln,
William Wallace, 1850-1862—Fiction. 2. United States—History—Civil War,
1861-1865—Fiction. 3. Time travel—Fiction. 4. Ghosts—Fiction.] I. Title.
PZ7.H2277 Gh 2001 [Fic]—dc21 99-462276

GHOSTS OF THE CIVIL WAR

SIMON & SCHUSTER BOOKS FOR YOUNG READERS

NEW YORK   LONDON   TORONTO   SYDNEY   SINGAPORE